This edition published by Parragon in 2009

Parragon
Queen Street House
4 Queen Street
Bath BA1 1HE, UK

ISBN 978-1-4075-8363-1
Printed in China

Fairy tales

Bath · New York · Singapore · Hong Kong · Cologne · Delhi · Melbourne

Sugarplum and the Butterfly

"Sugarplum," said the Fairy Queen, "I've got a very important job for you to do." Sugarplum was always given the most important work. The Fairy Queen said it was because she was the kindest and most helpful of all the fairies. "I want you to make a rose-petal ball gown for my birthday ball next week."

"It will be my pleasure," said Sugarplum happily.

Sugarplum began to gather cobwebs for the thread, and rose petals for the dress. While she was collecting the thread she found a butterfly caught in a cobweb.

"Oh, you poor thing," sighed Sugarplum. Very carefully, she untangled the butterfly, but his wing was broken. Sugarplum laid the butterfly on a bed of feathers. She gathered some nectar from a special flower and fed him a drop at a time. Then she began fixing his wing with a magic spell.

After six days, the butterfly was better. He was very grateful. But now Sugarplum was behind with her work!

"Oh dear! I shall never finish the Fairy Queen's ball gown by tomorrow," she cried. "Whatever shall I do?"

The butterfly comforted her. "Don't worry, Sugarplum," he

said. "We'll help you."

He gathered all his friends together. There were yellow, blue, red, and orange butterflies. He told them how Sugarplum had rescued him from the cobweb and helped to fix his wing.

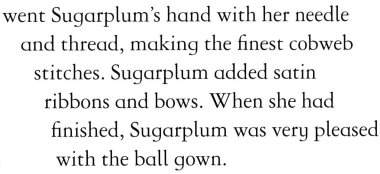

The butterflies gladly gathered up lots of rose petals and dropped them next to Sugarplum. Then the butterflies flew away to gather more cobwebs, while Sugarplum arranged all the petals. Back and forth went Sugarplum's hand with her needle and thread, making the finest cobweb stitches. Sugarplum added satin ribbons and bows. When she had finished, Sugarplum was very pleased with the ball gown.

"Dear friend," she said to the butterfly, "I couldn't have finished the dress without your help."

"And I could never have flown again without your kindness and help," said the butterfly.

And the Fairy Queen was delighted with her new ball gown!

The Midnight Fairies

Megan was staying with Grandma for a few days, while Mom was away.

Megan always had fun at Grandma's. But on the second night of Megan's visit, as she was getting ready for bed, Megan realized that she'd lost the pretty flower necklace Mom had given her. Megan and Grandma looked everywhere, but they couldn't find it.

Grandma gave Megan a hug. "Don't worry. We'll look in the yard tomorrow," she promised. "I'm sure it will be there."

Megan settled down to sleep, but she tossed and turned and finally woke up again. She couldn't stop thinking about her lost necklace.

Getting out of bed, she went to look out of the window. Somewhere in the distance, a clock chimed once... twice... twelve times. "Midnight!" Megan thought. Suddenly her eyes opened wide. At the bottom of the moonlit yard, where the wildflowers grew, lights began to wink and twinkle, and shimmering shapes danced in the air.

Fairies had come out to play! They danced and skipped through the air, laughing and flitting from flower to flower.

All at once Fairy Firefly spotted something—a silver necklace gleaming in the grass.

"Look!" she said to her fairy friends. "I wonder who this belongs to!"

"Maybe it's that little girl's," said Nightingale, pointing up to the window where Megan was looking out. "She looks very sad—as if she's lost something special."

"I wish we could make her smile again," said Moon Blossom.

The fairies looked at one another, and knew they were all thinking the same thing. First, they tucked the necklace safely behind a stone. Then, together, they flew across the yard and straight up to Megan's window.

As Megan gasped with amazement and delight, Stardust sprinkled her with glittering fairy dust.

"Now you'll be able to fly with us!" the fairies said happily.

With a fairy holding each hand, Megan whooshed out of the window and flew down to the bottom of the yard. When they landed, Stardust introduced herself and her friends. "We are the Midnight Fairies," she explained. "Every night at

midnight, we come out to dance and play in the moonlight. Will you be our friend and play with us tonight?"

"Of course I will!" said Megan happily.

With the moon beaming down and the friendly stars twinkling above, Megan and the fairies danced among the wildflowers. The cool grass tickled Megan's toes, and the fairies' laughter sounded like tiny crystal bells. Megan laughed with them, and felt happier than she ever had before.

When Megan was too tired to dance anymore, Firefly said, "We have a surprise for you." She brought out Megan's necklace.

"My necklace!" cried Megan. "You found it! Thank you!"

As Firefly gave the necklace back, Stardust sprinkled magic fairy dust over it. A beautiful fairy appeared in place of the flower.

"Oh!" breathed Megan. "How wonderful. It's you! It's a Midnight Fairy!"

"Yes," said Firefly. "But please don't tell anyone how it got there, or we might lose our fairy magic."

"I promise!" replied Megan.

As she put on her

necklace, Megan realized that she could barely keep her eyes open. With the Midnight Fairies fluttering over her, she curled up under the oak tree and fell asleep... until the morning, when she woke up, snug in her cozy bed in Grandma's house!

"How did I get back here?" Megan wondered. "Was it just a dream?"

She reached up to her neck—and there was her necklace, right where it should be.

"Hello!" said Grandma cheerfully, opening the bedroom door.

"Grandma, look!" said Megan. "I have my necklace back! Did *you* find it?"

"No, dear," said Grandma, with a puzzled look. She peered down at the necklace. "Oh, how lovely!" she said. "I hadn't noticed the fairy before."

"The Midnight Fairies!" Megan thought to herself. "So it wasn't a dream, after all!"

"I wonder how your necklace got back here," said Grandma, scratching her head.

Megan, smiling as she looked out toward the garden, knew the answer. But it was a secret that belonged to her—to her and the Midnight Fairies, the wonderful, magical friends she would never, ever forget.

Grumpy Fairy

Misery didn't have any friends. It was her own fault—she was always grumbling. Willow, her niece, couldn't understand her. "Why do you always find fault with everybody?" she asked.

"Because everybody is so useless!" said her grumpy aunt.

One day Misery told the fairy who baked the bread, "Your bread is too soft. I like crusty bread."

"If that's your attitude," said the baker fairy, "bake your own bread!"

"I shall!" said Misery.

The next day she was rude to the fairy who mended her shoes.

"No one speaks to me like that!" said the cobbler fairy. "From now on you can mend your own shoes."

"I'll be glad to," said Misery grumpily.

Then she insulted the fairy who gathered honey from the bees.

"How dare you?" said the honey-gathering fairy. "I'm not staying here to be insulted. You can collect your own honey."

"How are you going to manage?" Willow asked Misery.

"No problem," said Misery. "I'll do everything myself." And with that she got to work to bake some bread. Misery mixed and kneaded the dough and left it to rise. Then she put the loaf in the oven and sat down for a well-earned rest. Soon she had

dozed off.

She was woken by a smell of burning. All that was left of the loaf of bread were a few burnt cinders. What Misery didn't realize was that the baker fairy used a special baking spell—a spell that Misery didn't know!

Misery went to gather some honey. She waved her arms at the bees buzzing around the hive, shouting, "Out of my way, bees." They didn't like it one little

bit! Their answer was to swarm around her and sting her. You see, what Misery didn't know was that the honey fairy used a special honey-gathering spell.

Misery ran from the bees as fast as she could. As she did, she broke her shoe! Oh dear! What a state she was in! Burnt bread, bee stings, and only one shoe!

"You can't go on like this," said Willow when she saw Misery.

Misery did some serious thinking. "Tell all the fairies I've turned over a new leaf," she told Willow. "From now on I won't be grumpy anymore."

Willow was delighted! Misery didn't complain about anything for months after that, and Willow kept her fingers crossed that it would last.

Lazy Fairy Daisy

Daisy was a fairy
Who was lazy as can be.
Whenever someone asked for help,
She'd yawn and say, "Why me?"

When other fairies teased her,
And called her lazybones,
She'd mutter, "Words can't hurt me.
They're not like sticks and stones."

Why she was so idle,
It was quite hard to say.
(The only reason was, I fear,
That she was born that way!)

So while the others rushed around
Preparing for the ball,
Daisy lounged around and yawned,
"What's the matter with you all?"

She watched them as they cut and stitched,
To make each fancy dress.
But Daisy didn't lend a hand.
She just could not care less!

Even Princess Lucy,
Who liked to dream a lot,
Had made herself a ball gown,
But Daisy just would not!

The night before the summer ball
Poor Daisy saw her fate.
"I don't have a dress to wear,
And now it is too late!"

"Don't worry," whispered Lucy,
Who had a bright idea.
"I'll promise that you'll have a dress.
Now wipe away that tear."

Soon Daisy's friends were busy.
They stitched throughout the night,
Until they'd made a ball gown
That fitted her just right.

"Oh, thank you!" exclaimed Daisy,
Smiling now with pleasure.
"Today I've learned a lesson—
One that I'll always treasure!

For when there is a job to do,
Now I understand.
The work is done in half the time
If we all lend a hand!

I won't be lazy anymore,
Not when there's work to do!
So when this ball is over
I'll tidy up for you!"

Clumsy Fairy

Clumsy Clementine was the worst in her dance class at Fairy School.

"Clementine! Feathers, not elephants!" Madam Bouquet, the dance teacher, would say.

At the end of the term all the fairies were given a special task for the break.

"Clementine," said Madam Bouquet, "your job is to paint this rose-petal lotion on a little girl called Alice's spots every night to make them better."

That night Clementine flew in through Alice's window. So far so good! But then clumsy Clementine knocked over a vase...

Alice woke up. "Who's there?" she asked sleepily.

"It's Clementine," said the fairy. She explained why she had come. "You're not really supposed to see me," she added.

"Can you really do magic?" Alice asked Clementine.

"Yes," Clementine told her. "I'm good at magic. But I'm so clumsy!" She told Alice about her dance classes and Alice told Clementine about her ballet lessons.

"I'll help you with your dancing if you like," Alice said to Clementine.

By the end of the week Alice's spots were gone, and Clementine could pirouette.

Madam Bouquet couldn't believe her eyes. "Clementine," she gasped, "what happened?"

"It must be magic!" smiled Clementine.

The Yellow Bluebells

The fairies at Corner Cottage were always busy looking after the flowers in the yard.

It was Blossom's job to paint the bluebells blue.

One evening, Blossom had a cold. "I don't think I can work tonight," she told her friend Petal, sniffing. "I'll have to ask the gnomes."

"No problem!" said Chip and Chuck when she asked them. "Just leave it to us."

When Blossom got up the next morning she was feeling much better—until she saw that the naughty gnomes had painted some of the bluebells… *yellow!*

"Have you seen what they've done?" she said to Petal. "What will Jamie think?"

Jamie lived in Corner Cottage. That morning when he came out to play he noticed that something looked different.

"I'm sure those flowers were blue yesterday," he thought.

"Mom," he said, going into the kitchen, "I've picked you some flowers."

"Yellowbells?" said Mom. "I don't remember planting those."

That night, Blossom painted all the bluebells blue again. When Jamie and his mom went into the yard the next morning, everything was as it should be.

"It must have been fairies!" joked Mom.

Twinkle the Tooth Fairy

Twinkle the Tooth Fairy was always very busy. Every night, she collected the baby teeth that the children left under their pillows. But the teeth were so tiny they were difficult to find in the dark.

Late one summer evening, Twinkle was looking for the last baby tooth of the night. Finally she found it and put her last shiny coin under the pillow.

"Good night," whispered Twinkle as she gently kissed the sleeping child and flew silently out of the window. The sun was just coming up as Twinkle flew back to Fairyland.

All the fairies in Fairyland were very busy getting ready for the Fairy Ball. Fairy food had to be made by the best fairy cooks. Hundreds of fairy lights had to be put up. And the fairy orchestra was practicing very hard.

Before going to bed, Twinkle decided to go and see her friend Thimble, the fairy dressmaker. Thimble had been busy too, making all the dresses for the Fairy Ball.

"What beautiful dresses!" exclaimed Twinkle.

"I'm glad you like them," said Thimble. "But they would be so much better if I could decorate them with golden thread. I can't find any in all of Fairyland."

"I know where there's lots of golden thread. Leave it to me," Twinkle said excitedly, and she flew off high into the sky.

Soon, she was among hundreds of bright, shining stars. On she flew, until she reached a huge golden ball—the Sun.

"Please, Mr. Sun," she asked, "can you spare some of your fine golden thread for my friend Thimble?"

Twinkle waited. All of a sudden, a long trail of golden thread came slowly from the center of the sun. Twinkle took the end of it, and began to pull it toward her.

"That tickles!" laughed the Sun.

Twinkle had soon gathered a large bundle of the precious thread. "Thank you, Mr. Sun," she said.

"You're very welcome, Twinkle," chuckled the sun.

When Thimble saw what Twinkle had brought her, she clapped her hands with joy!

"Thank you, Twinkle!" she said. "Now my dresses will be perfect. And I promise you will have the finest dress of all for the ball."

"I've never been to the Fairy Ball," said Twinkle quietly.

"Why ever not?" asked Thimble curiously.

"It takes me such a long time to

find all the children's teeth, I never get back in time," Twinkle said sadly.

"Don't you worry. I'll think of something!" said Thimble.

Twinkle felt very tired after her busy night and went straight to bed. When she woke up the next day, she was surprised to see a large bag at the foot of her bed.

Inside the bag were the most beautiful purple and gold velvet purses. Pinned to the bag was a note, which read:

Dear Twinkle,

I have made these special purses from the leftover fairy dress cloth. The children can put their teeth into them. The purses will be much easier for you to find in the dark. With a bit of luck, you will be back in time for the ball!

Your best fairy friend, Thimble

Later that evening, Twinkle collected all the children's baby

teeth as usual. She left each child with a shiny coin tucked into one of the purses, which she carefully placed under their pillows. Twinkle whispered to each sleeping child, "Please use the purse to keep your next baby tooth safe."

A few days later it was the night of the Fairy Ball. Twinkle was very excited. She so hoped that she'd be back in time to join in the fun! But first she had her important job to do.

When she flew off that night to collect the baby teeth, Twinkle was overjoyed to see that each child had put their baby tooth inside their purse. Now they were easy to find!

She kissed each child and whispered, "Thank you!"

After gathering all the teeth up carefully, Twinkle flew quickly back to Fairyland. When she was nearly home, she

could hear the sounds of the fairy orchestra in the distance. The whole sky was lit up with the lights of the Fairy Ball.

"It's already started!" she thought, flying even faster.

When she reached home, Twinkle rushed to see Thimble.

"Am I too late?" she asked breathlessly.

"It's only just begun!" laughed Thimble.

Twinkle had a wonderful time at the Fairy Ball. And everyone agreed that in her beautiful new dress, she was the prettiest fairy of all.

Clever Fairy Heather

Heather was the smartest
Of the fairies in the land.
So people always came to her—
She loved to lend a hand.

No matter what the problem was,
Whatever it involved,
As soon as Heather tackled it,
You knew it would be solved.

"Don't you worry!" she would smile,
As helpful as can be.
"I will find an answer.
Just you wait and see!"

Now Heather had her problems, too,
And ones she longed to share.
But nobody would take the time—
They did not seem to care.

When Heather tried to tell her friends
About her little troubles,
All they seemed to want to do
Was talk of their own muddles.

Heather, though a patient girl,
Finally slammed her door.
She shouted in her loudest voice,
"I won't listen anymore!"

The other fairies were amazed.
"Has Heather gone on strike?
It really isn't like her …
It's just not Heather-like!"

Then Daisy saw just what was wrong,
"Oh, now I understand!
When Heather has a problem,
Who gives a helping hand?"

Lily blushed a shade of pink.
"I really must agree.
Because I don't say thank you
Whenever she helps me."

"It's time that we said thank you
For all her good advice,
And showed her just how much we care
By doing something nice."

So Lily gave her bluebells,
And polished Heather's wings.
While lazy Daisy cleaned her home
And fixed some broken things.

"I might be clever," Heather said,
And hugged them happily.
"But not enough to realize
What friends you are to me!"

Rain, Rain, Go Away!

It was a rainy day, and Raindrop the fairy liked the rain.

"Come and play outside," Raindrop said to the other fairies.

The other fairies did not like the rain. "It's too wet to play outside," they said.

All the fairies lived at the bottom of a garden that belonged to Ann and Tom.

Ann and Tom looked out of the window.

"I'm bored," said Ann.

"It's too wet to play outside," said Tom.

"I'm tired of being inside," said Ann.

Down at the bottom of the garden, Raindrop had started to cry because no one wanted to play with her. And the more Raindrop cried, the more it rained. Soon it was pouring!

Sunny the sunshine fairy looked at the rain. "Don't cry, Raindrop," she said. "I will play with you."

Raindrop stopped crying. Like magic, the rain stopped. The sun came out.

Ann and Tom came out to play in the garden.

"Look! A beautiful rainbow!" they said.

Too Much Sun

It was a hot sunny day. Tom and Ann were too hot to play. They lay on the sofa and watched TV. Even the flowers in the garden were wilting in the hot sun.

"It's just too hot!" said Ann.

But Sunny the sunshine fairy, down at the bottom of Ann and Tom's garden, liked the sun. The hotter the better!

"Come and play in the sky," she said to her fairy friends.

Sunny, Windy, and Raindrop flew up into the sky. The fairies started to play hide-and-seek.

First Sunny hid in the clouds. Then Windy blew the clouds away.

Then Raindrop waved her wand at a cloud and it began to rain. She hid in the shower of rain until Windy blew the raincloud away with a laugh.

The flowers in Ann and Tom's garden lifted up their petals gratefully when the refreshing shower of rain came down.

Now it was not too hot anymore. It was a lovely day and everything was sparkling from the shower of rain.

Tom and Ann were not too hot any more.

"Let's go and play in the yard!" said Tom.